kress

kress

KITOTO
THE
MIGHTY

TOLOLWA M. MOLLEL
KRISTI FROST

Stoddart
Kids

TORONTO • NEW YORK

*Stoddart Publishing gratefully acknowledges the support
of the Canada Council and the Ontario Arts Council
in the development of writing and publishing in Canada.*

Published in Canada in 1998 by
Stoddart Kids,
a division of Stoddart Publishing Co. Limited
34 Lesmill Road
Toronto, Canada M3B 2T6
Tel (416) 445-3333 Fax (416) 445-5967
E-mail Customer.Service@ccmailgw.genpub.com

Published in the United States in 1998 by
Stoddart Kids
a division of Stoddart Publishing Co. Limited
180 Varick Street, 9th Floor
New York, New York 14207
Toll free 1-800-805-1083
E-mail gdsinc@genpub.com

Distributed in Canada by
General Distribution Services
30 Lesmill Road
Toronto, Canada M3B 2T6
Tel (416) 445-3333 Fax (416) 445-5967
E-mail Customer.Service@ccmailgw.genpub.com

Distributed in the United States by
General Distribution Services
85 River Rock Drive, Suite 202
Buffalo, New York 14207
Toll free 1-800-805-1083
E-mail gdsinc@genpub.com

Canadian Cataloguing in Publication Data

Mollel, Tololwa M. (Tololwa Marti)
Kitoto the mighty

ISBN 0-7737-3019-2

1. Mice — Folklore.   2. Tales — Africa.
I. Frost, Kristi.   II. Title.

PS8576.0451K57 1997   j398.2'096045293233   C96-932304-2
PZ8.1.M73Ki 1997

Printed and bound in Hong Kong, China by
Book Art Inc., Toronto

High in the sky, a hawk circled and searched. Then, swift as an arrow, he dropped to the ground.

Barely ahead of the hawk's claws, Kitoto darted into a bush. The little mouse who had never learned to dig burrows hid there, with nothing to eat all day.

The next morning, before the sun was up or the hawk awoke, Kitoto scurried hungrily across the Savannah. He found a fallen baobab fruit. But another creature had seen it first, and the delicious seeds were gone.

That is when the hungry little mouse heard the sound of a big, rushing river. Cautiously, he approached the riverbank and watched the angry water sweep away huge trees and rocks.

"How powerful the river is!" thought Kitoto. And he had an idea.

"I am Kitoto the Mouse, small and weak," he cried to the river. "I wish to make friends with you. With a friend like you to protect me, I won't have to go hungry for fear of the hawk. You must be the most powerful of all beings."

"Not so," roared the river. "The sun can protect you better for he is far more powerful than I. He burns me to a trickle in the dry season. The sun is the most powerful being."

The river wove a beautiful nest of steam, placed Kitoto inside, and gently blew it above the trees and mountains, into the soft sunlight.

"Why, I am bigger than the Savannah!" Kitoto marveled, as the earth below grew smaller and smaller. He felt very pleased with himself. Still, he had never in his life imagined making friends with one as powerful as the sun.

"I must do my best to impress him," Kitoto decided, as he arrived at the sun's home late in the day.

Sparks swirled as the weary sun stoked and fanned his dying log fire.

Kitoto puffed himself up importantly. "I am Kitoto the Mighty, Master of the Savannah," he announced. "I wish to make friends with the most powerful being. I thought it was the river. But no, the river tells me it is you."

The sun, wrapped in a blanket, shivered in the chill of dusk. "Not so," he replied. "There is one far more powerful than I, who gathers the clouds and hides the Savannah from my view. The wind is the most powerful being."

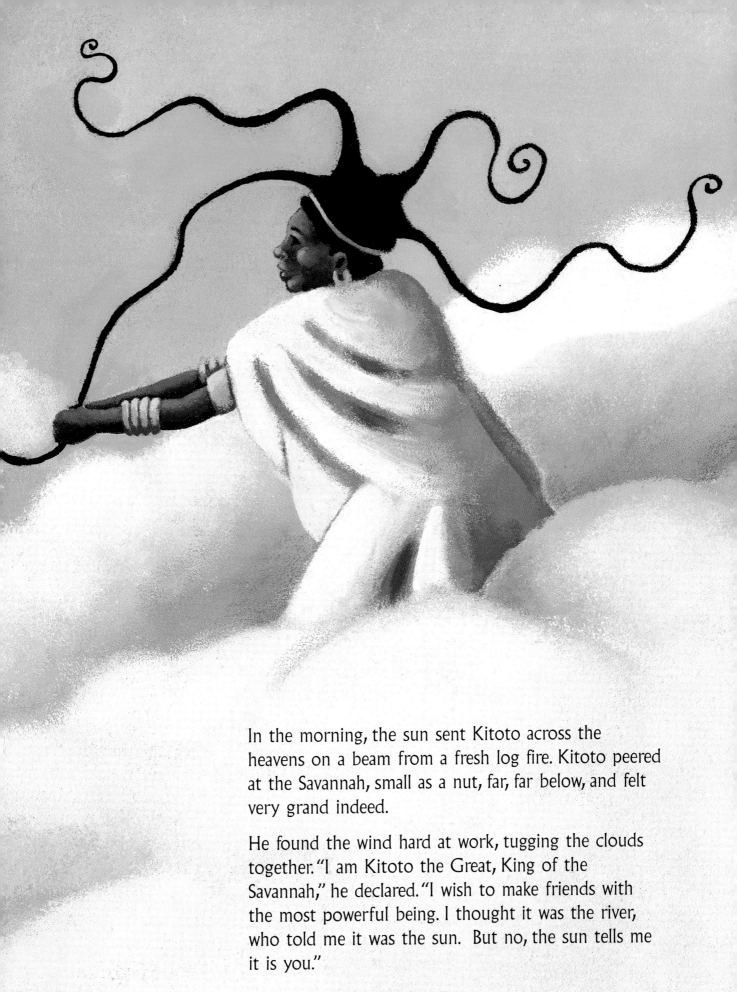

In the morning, the sun sent Kitoto across the
heavens on a beam from a fresh log fire. Kitoto peered
at the Savannah, small as a nut, far, far below, and felt
very grand indeed.

He found the wind hard at work, tugging the clouds
together. "I am Kitoto the Great, King of the
Savannah," he declared. "I wish to make friends with
the most powerful being. I thought it was the river,
who told me it was the sun. But no, the sun tells me
it is you."

"Not so," replied the wind. "There is one far more powerful than I, one I cannot tug with my strong braids, however hard I try. The mountain is the most powerful being."

With the longest of her braids, the wind swung Kitoto away to a distant mountain peak.

"I am Kitoto the Magnificent, Emperor of the Savannah," the little mouse proclaimed to the mountain. "I wish to make friends with the most powerful being. I thought it was the river, who told me it was the sun, who told me it was the wind. But no, the wind tells me it is you."

"Not so," thundered the majestic mountain. "There is one far more powerful than I, who chomps away at my root. Surely this creature, whom I have felt but never seen, must be the most powerful being of all."

Then the mountain rumbled and opened wide, allowing Kitoto to enter.

Down, down Kitoto scampered, through dark pathways, deep to the root of the mountain. There, he found himself in a huge maze of tunnels, archways, halls, and chambers. The walls were cool and smooth and smelled pleasantly. Tiny, shiny pebbles lit the way.

At every bend, Kitoto expected to see a giant loom before him, for a giant it must be, he thought, to carve such a world out of the mountain.

A sound from the shadows startled him.

In his fear, Kitoto forgot to be Mighty or Great, Master, King or Emperor. "Please do not harm me," he pleaded with the unseen giant. "It is only Kitoto the Mouse, small and weak. I wish to make friends with you, the most powerful of all beings. With you to protect me I won't have to go hungry for fear of the hawk." Kitoto waited, trembling.

From the shadows, a figure stepped forward.

Kitoto stared in amazement as the figure bowed.

"I am Kigego, the mountain mouse. Welcome to my home."

"*Your* home? *You* built all this?" Kitoto asked. "The paths, the tunnels . . . *everything?*"

"Everything," replied Kigego. "With nothing more than my teeth and a lot of hard work." Her eyes glowed proudly. "Come."

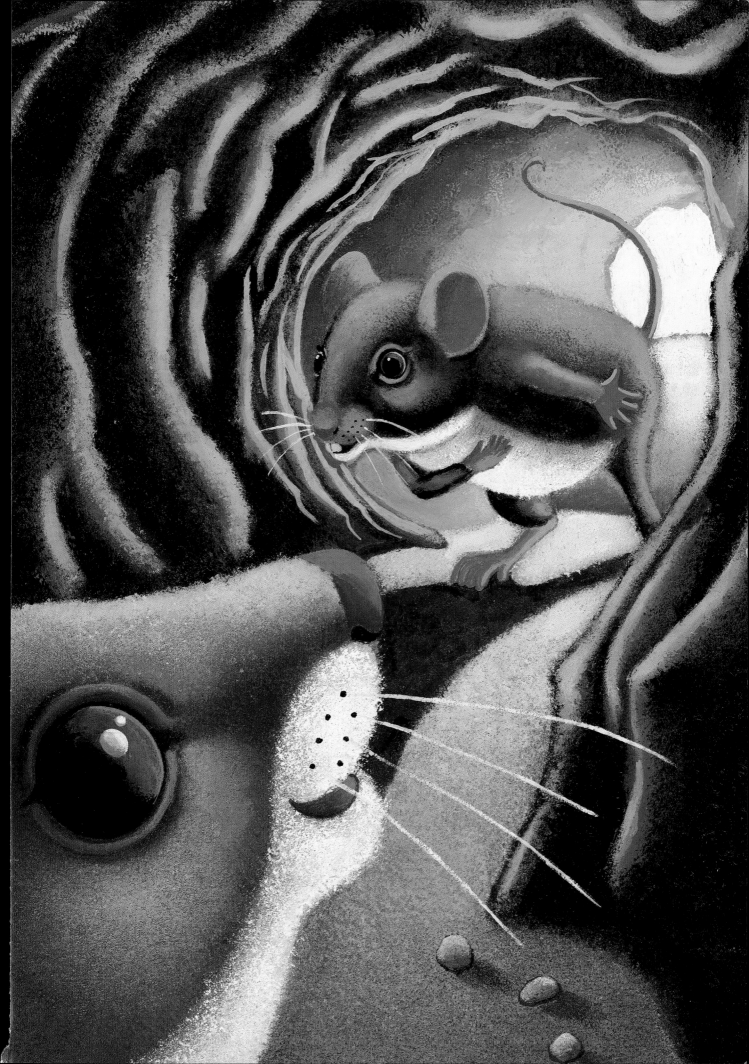

Like old friends, the two mice explored the winding pathways.
They enjoyed a game of hide and seek in the mazes.
They played catch with shiny pebbles.
Then they fell asleep on cushions of soft earth.

When they awoke, Kigego unearthed a sumptuous hoard of bulbs, tubers, and roots. "I'll teach you the secrets of the ground," she promised, chuckling.

Kitoto chuckled back and said, "And I will teach you the secrets of the Savannah."

High in the sky, a hawk circled and searched. Deep at the root of
a mountain, two friends chewed merrily away. And after the
hawk had gone to sleep, they ventured out to enjoy the sweet,
cool night air.

To this very day, few would guess that the mouse is the most powerful being on the big, wide Savannah. But the rushing river, the weary sun, the tugging wind — even the majestic mountain, will tell you this is so.

AUTHOR'S NOTE

Kitoto the Mighty is my version of a traditional folk tale found the world over. In the tale, a mouse searches the universe for a fitting bride — the most powerful being of all. My version differs from the traditional tale in one major respect. In *Kitoto the Mighty* it is self-preservation, not romance, that prompts the mouse, Kitoto (Key toh TOH), to seek out the most powerful being — Kigego (Key geh GOH). There is, therefore, no wedding at the end in my version, only a union of strengths and a promise of friendship. This shift, which I found necessary in order to create an original telling, brought about a new character — the hawk — and a change in the nature of Kitoto's journey. However, like the traditional tale, *Kitoto the Mighty* deals with the theme of hidden strength; the weakest proves to be the most powerful being.